For Joyce who braved the skunks after dark with me, for Hope who believed in Cordelia when she was still just a whisper in my ear... and for every one of us who has been knocked down to the ground, but chose to get back up - to become the hero of our own story.

– MNS

Kane Miller, A Division of EDC Publishing

Text and illustrations copyright © Michelle Nelson-Schmidt 2016

For information contact:
Kane Miller, A Division of EDC Publishing
PO Box 470663
Tulsa, OK 74147-0663
www.kanemiller.com
www.edcpub.com
www.usbornebooksandmore.com

Library of Congress Control Number: 2015954205

Manufactured by Regent Publishing Services, Hong Kong
Printed September 2016 in ShenZhen, Guangdong, China

Hardcover ISBN: 978-1-61067-442-3
Paperback ISBN: 978-1-61067-441-6

Cordelia

Michelle Nelson-Schmidt

Kane Miller
A DIVISION OF EDC PUBLISHING

Cordelia could fly along with the breeze.

What seemed impossible, she did with ease.

the higher she flew.

the higher she went,

and confidence grew,

The deeper her courage

From the top of her head, to the tips of her toes,
the more she believed, the more that she rose.

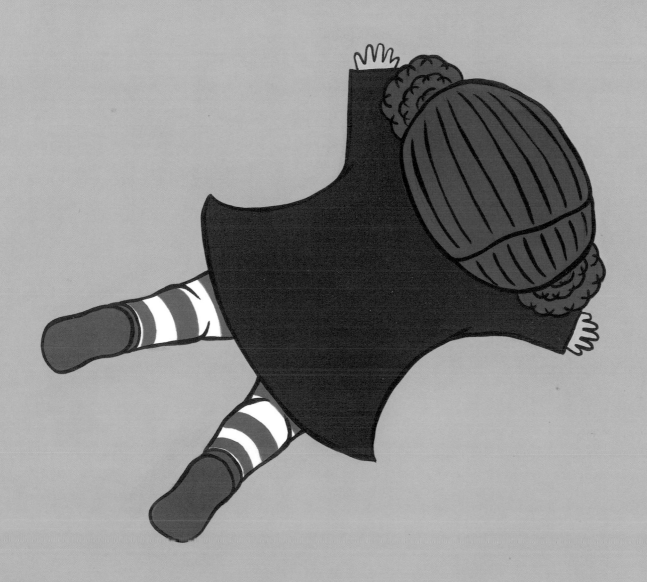

Cordelia could fly, she always just knew.
This faith in herself was how it was true.

When she trusted her heart and trusted it whole,
she could sing with the birds, songs filling her soul.

From up overhead, the earth sparkled and gleamed,
a world filled with friends, with magic and dreams.

Up in the sky, she would make the moon smile,
dance with the stars, and laugh all the while.

Cordelia's world was vivid, colored and bright.
Joy filled her days. Beauty filled her nights.

Her happiness was endless; her delight only grew ...

until the day others doubted she flew.

They didn't see her sing and play.
They didn't see her fly.
No one would believe her.
They didn't even try.

She used lots of ways –
as many as she could find –
to explain what was possible.
But no one changed their mind.

No one seemed to listen,
no one seemed to care,
when Cordelia explained
how she flew in the air.

They said that she was silly. They said that she was wrong.
They made Cordelia doubt who she'd been all along.

As their words filled her head, her heart began to sink.
Does who you are depend on what other people think?

So Cordelia stopped doing the thing that she loved,
the thing that made her happy - that made her who she was.

She didn't fly and sing with the birds in the trees.
No twirling, spinning, smiling; no gliding on the breeze.

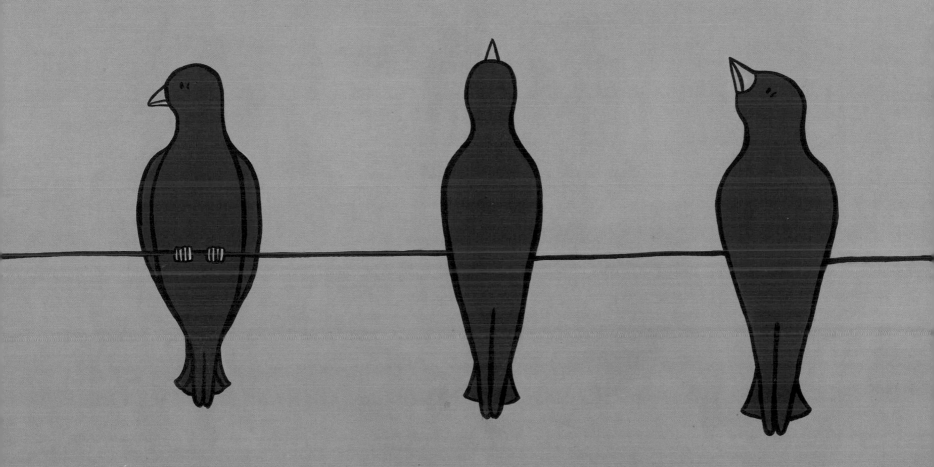

She didn't wish good morning to the whale in the salty air, as the sun warmed her skin, and the wind blew her hair.

She didn't visit the moon to try to make him grin,
or play games with the stars, seeing who would win.

Cordelia began to walk,
in an ordinary way.

Like everybody else,

on an ordinary day.

As the days passed, Cordelia stayed on the ground.
Life became gray – there was no color; there was no sound.

She missed the stars and the moon.
She missed the bird's sweet song.
She missed the mighty whale – everything was wrong.

As she thought about her friends, her sadness became anger.
She was mad at herself for letting other people change her.

Who was anyone to say, if she could or couldn't fly?
What was or wasn't possible - if they didn't even try?

With confidence and strength, Cordelia began anew.
She was the girl who could fly, and she knew that this was true.

a feeling began to start.

As Cordelia ran along,

a healing in her heart.

It was a soothing of her soul,

She remembered who she was and that she loved to fly.
As the doubts of others fell away, she rose into the sky.

Cordelia began to fly again – to sing and play and soar.
Because what others thought, didn't matter anymore.

She knew just who she was, knew who she could be.
And this belief in herself, set Cordelia free.

Just because another can't see this world like you,
doesn't make things impossible, or mean they are not true.